SHABAZZ LARKIN

THE THING ABOUT BEES

A Love Letter ♡

Readers to Eaters

SAN FRANCISCO, CA

NOTE TO READERS

**There are more than 20,000 species of bees in the world.
The fuzzy round bees in this book are bumble bees. They make honey like
honey bees do, but in small, jumbled nests. The neat and tidy honeycombs
you see in this book are honey-bee honeycombs.**

READERS to EATERS
San Francisco, CA
readerstoeaters.com

Distributed by Publishers Group West
Printed in the USA by Worzalla, Stevens Point, WI (5/19)

Text and illustrations copyright © 2019 by Shabazz Larkin

Book production by The Kids at Our House
Special thanks to Karin Snelson and Red Herring Design of our bee team

Shabazz Larkin choreographed a series of posed photos of himself and his family—
all taken in Nashville, Tennessee—to create the illustrations for this book.
He was inspired by the techniques of two of his favorite American artists,
Kehinde Wiley and Norman Rockwell.

The text is set in Brown.

10 9 8 7 6 5 4 3 2 1
First Edition

Cataloging-in-Publication Data is on file at the Library of Congress
ISBN: 978-0-9980477-9-9

FSC
www.fsc.org

MIX
Paper from
responsible sources
FSC® C002589

THIS BOOK IS DEDICATED TO MY SONS WHO TEACH ME WHAT IT MEANS TO BE FEARLESS.

-SHABAZZ

② As the bee drinks the flower's nectar, she gets pollen all over her hairy body!

③ The bee moves pollen from one flower to another.

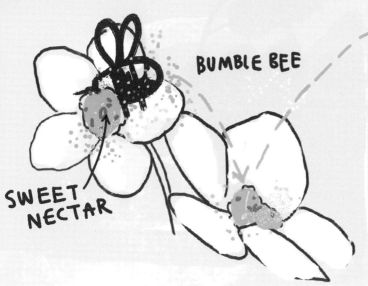

BUMBLE BEE

SWEET NECTAR

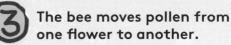

⑥ ... AND PRESTO!

The flower turns into a fruit you can eat.

STRAWBERRIES

⑦ THIS PROCESS IS CALLED POLLINATION

We'd be hungry without the bees. They help vegetables and nuts grow, too.

THANK YOU, BEES!

Here's the thing about bees.

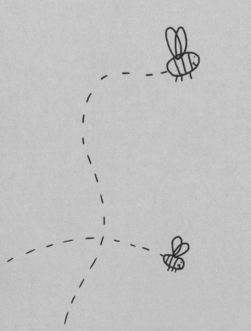

Sometimes bees can be a bit rude.
They fly in your face and prance on your food.
They buzz in the bushes and buzz in your ear.

They sneak up behind you
and fill you with fear.

BUZZZZ Z Z Z Z Z Z

And worst of all, they do this thing
called sting.

O U C H !

OH NOOOO!

We may want bees gone
        because their sting hurts.
But if they were all gone,
        it would hurt much worse.

WITHOUT BEES...

there'd be no more picnics with watermelon.
There'd be no more smoothies with mango.
There'd be no more strawberries for shortcakes.
And no more avocados for tacos.

There'd be no apples,
     which means no more pie.
No more cucumbers,
     which means no more pickles.
No more blueberries and raspberries for pancakes
     or sweet cherries to drizzle.

Because some foods won't grow
without bees to help them along.

IN A WAY,
THE BEES ARE
JUST LIKE YOU!

You.

YOU buzz in the bushes
and buzz in my ear.

YOU sneak up behind me
and fill me with fear.

YOU fly in my face
and prance on my food.

YOU even sting,
when you're in a bad mood.

But I never stop

loving ♡

you.

You're my sweet cherry.
The apple pie of my eye.
You're my cucumber pickle.
My bumble bee in the sky.
You're my cold watermelon
at a picnic in the park.
You're the avocados on my tacos...

You're my strawberry heart.

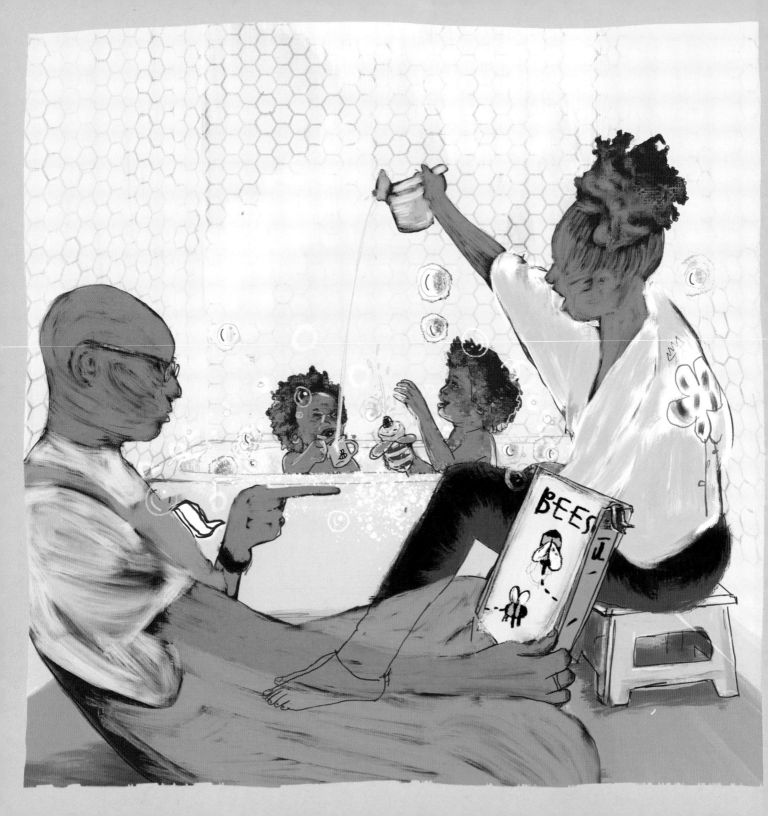

Without those little buzzers,
the world wouldn't know what to do.

That's the thing about bees.
We need them just as much
as we need you.

I HAVE A LOT TO LEARN FROM BEES

I wrote this book because I have a ridiculous fear of bees. When my sons were born I didn't want to pass that fear to them. So I set out to discover all I could about the little buzzers.

I learned three things about bees. First, I learned that every living creature has a special part to play in the world, and that includes you. Second, when I learn more about a scary thing, the thing feels less scary to me. Third, I researched which bees and wasps are kind and which are kinda mean. I made a guide to help you see the difference, too.

It's brave to try to understand the things that scare us.
Now, go be brave.

Love,
SHABAZZ

EVERYTHING YOU NEED TO KNOW ABOUT HOW <u>NOT</u> TO GET STUNG

A GUIDE TO BEES (AND WASPS) FROM KIND TO KINDA MEAN

BEES ⤵

BUMBLE BEE

* the friendliest of all bees
* can sting, but usually ignores humans
* nests in the ground
* excellent pollinator
* makes honey, but not nearly as much as honey bees
* very fuzzy
* too big and blobby for its tiny wings, but flies anyhow

CARPENTER BEE

* a BIG harmless bee
* rarely stings
* makes nests in dead wood, like in old logs or in your house (that's why it's called a carpenter bee)
* great pollinator
* has a little furry jacket

POLLINATOR: Anything—like a bee, bird, butterfly or bat—that helps fruits and vegetables grow by spreading pollen from plant to plant.

HONEY BEE

* the world's best pollinator (and pollen eater)
* very friendly
* can only sting ONCE
* lives inside hollow trees or logs (or in human-built hives)
* makes honey, and then eats it
* makes wax to build honeycombs (for storing pollen, honey and baby bees)
* does a waggle dance to help hive-mates find the good flowers

KIND ───────

BEE SAFETY & ETIQUETTE

STAY CALM and hold still if a bee comes around.

AVOID carrying ripe mangos, or you will smell like bee dinner.

DON'T FORGET Bees don't want to sting you, they are busy collecting pollen.

WEAR A HAT if you don't like bees in your hair.

IGNORE bees in flight. They can't sting you if they are not on you.

NEVER SWAT at bees. They will sting you if you do.

WEAR SHOES Some bees make nests in the ground.

TELL AN ADULT right away if a bee stings you.

WASPS →

MUD DAUBER

* this little buzzer is not a bee
* not aggressive, rarely stings
* has a long skinny body with almost no hair
* hunts spiders for dinner
* most famous for its tube-shaped nests made out of mud
* not a pollinator

HORNET

* the largest wasp
* only aggressive when threatened
* sting hurts the most of all wasps, and they can sting more than once
* a pollinator, but much less so than bees
* chews wood into a pulp to make paper nests
* loves to eat rotting fruit and other insects

YELLOW JACKET

* very aggressive when threatened
* not very hairy
* also not a bee, but they do pollinate a bit
* if you see one, walk away slowly
* if one stings you, run away fast, because others will follow
* hunts garden pests, making gardeners happy
* eats meat and people food, making picnickers grumpy

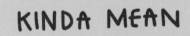

KINDA MEAN